# MR. BEAN'S HOLIDAY

# The World According to BEAN

Designed by
Christina Quintero

PRICE STERN SLOAN
Published by the Penguin Group
Penguin Group (USA) Inc., 375 Hudson Street, New York, New York 10014, U.S.A.
Penguin Group (Canada), 90 Eglinton Avenue East, Suite 700, Toronto, Ontario, Canada M4P 2Y3
(a division of Pearson Penguin Canada Inc.)
Penguin Books Ltd, 80 Strand, London WC2R 0RL, England
Penguin Ireland, 25 St Stephen's Green, Dublin 2, Ireland
(a division of Penguin Books Ltd)
Penguin Group (Australia), 250 Camberwell Road, Camberwell, Victoria 3124, Australia
(a division of Pearson Australia Group Pty Ltd)
Penguin Books India Pvt Ltd, 11 Community Centre, Panchsheel Park, New Delhi - 110 017, India
Penguin Group (NZ), 67 Apollo Drive, Mairangi Bay, Auckland 1311, New Zealand
(a division of Pearson New Zealand Ltd)
Penguin Books (South Africa) (Pty) Ltd, 24 Sturdee Avenue, Rosebank, Johannesburg 2196, South Africa

Penguin Books Ltd, Registered Offices:
80 Strand, London WC2R 0RL, England

www.mrbeansholiday.net

Library of Congress Control Number: 2006038304

ISBN 978-0-8431-2524-5                    10 9 8 7 6 5 4 3 2 1

# MR. BEAN'S HOLIDAY

## The World According to BEAN

### Mr. Bean's Photo Album

By Rebecca McCarthy

Based the original character created by
Rowan Atkinson and Richard Curtis

Based on the motion picture screenplay by
Hamish McColl and Robin Driscoll

PSS!
PRICE STERN SLOAN

Welcome to beautiful, sunny, merry old England!

This is where people come to find **tea, the Queen, and Platform $9\frac{3}{4}$**. If you want directions to England from your house, I can tell you how to do it. Walk out of America and turn right, then go straight across the ocean until you get to ~~dry~~ land.

Normally my home is lovely, with Mrs. Wicket's flowers in the window, but today she has had to take them inside due to a **bit of rain**. Actually, for two weeks she has had to take them inside due to a **bit of rain**. In fact, perhaps today isn't the best day for me to show you all of the sights in England, due to a bit of . . . well, you know.

Mr. Bean
c/o Mrs. Wicket
Daffodils
12 Arbor Road, Highbury
London N10, England

The Queen lives somewhere over here in a lovely castle.

Enough! Enough rain already! Stop it!

"Wee-wee this" and "Wee-wee that."

CANNES

This is Teddy.

But I can't complain. I had a brilliant stroke of luck today. See, I won a trip to the beach. This particular beach is in Cannes, France. So see you later, rain!

I've **never met a French person**, but I'm sure they are lovely people because they invented **French bread, French toast, French dressing**, and they enjoy talking about wee-wee, which is very silly. Sometimes they show French films on telly and all you hear is "Wee-wee this" and "Wee-wee that." **Funny people!** They spell it differently from the English, though—*oui*.

Yes, Cannes will be the perfect place for me to **take my holiday**. I've got some money in the freezer that I've been saving for a rainy day, and this is about as rainy a day as I've ever seen.

I CAN go to Cannes. Hee-hee!

# An interview with the great independent filmmaker Mr. Bean

**Q:** When did you begin your career as an independent filmmaker?

**A:** Not four minutes ago. I've decided to film my holiday and then graciously allow the viewing public to view it.

**Q:** Where did you receive your training?

**A:** The salesperson taught me all about the zoom lens. It took an eternity to learn—twenty minutes at least—but looking back now I don't feel that any of that time was wasted. Education really is the most important thing.

**Q:** Do you practice any other arts?

**A:** Oh yes. Just last year I practiced writing poetry, a lot, in Miss Rosemary Hosebury's poetry class down at the library. I'm really quite good. I also studied dance with a *Miss Ermentrude's Learn the Two-Step and Other Social Dances* videotape that I was lucky enough to find in the bargain bin at the local video store. And as a child I spent many hours play-acting with Teddy, having pretend tea parties and such. I don't really consider acting an art, however. Anybody can do it.

**Q:** What do you hope to accomplish with this film?

**A:** To make heaps of money. Of course I hope to inspire people, bring about world peace, make the children of the world join hands and sing in harmony, but mostly I want to make heaps of money.

*Mostly I want to make heaps of money.*

Being a creative, free-thinking, spontaneous, and fun *artiste* requires lots of planning, and, as you can see, I made this chart of my holiday plan.

I shall spend nine and one half hours traveling to the beach, eighty-four hours having the time of my life at the beach, and nine and one half hours on the journey home. With such well-laid-out plans, what could possibly go wrong?

# THE HERO BEGINS HIS JOURNEY

I'm going on vacation to Cannes
To sit on the beach and get tannes
I will meet every woman and mannes
Named Pierre or Amélie or Dannes
I won't be driving a vannes to Cannes
And I won't say I walked or I rannes
I'll go by train and by taxi, with map in hannds
And make a movie for all of my fannes!

P.S. Hit on the head with a frying pannes.
(I don't know where to fit this in the poem,
but this line is too good to lose.)

# How to Prepare Your Home for Holiday

1. Situate Teddy in front of the telly and turn it on. Teddy likes to watch a lot of telly, so turn the volume up very loud because if Mrs. Wicket decides to sing in the shower while the programme is on, Teddy will not be able to hear it.

2. Leave plenty of food out for Teddy. He'll need something from all the food groups, so set the table with heaps of fish, cheese, bananas, and ketchup.

3. Leave the window open so Teddy can get some fresh air.

4. Lock the front door to prevent any burglars from getting in. Put sign on the door telling burglars that the door is shut tight and they'll have no luck budging it, but perhaps they'll want to try down the hall in No. 3, because the man in there hides the key under the welcome mat.

5. Turn the hot water on so Teddy can make tea if he wants. Also turn on the electric blanket for those chilly nights. In case he gets wet from rain coming in from the open window, turn the hair-dryer on so he can dry off.

6. **REMEMBER TO TURN OFF THE IRON!!! VERY DANGEROUS TO LEAVE THE IRON ON WHILE YOU'RE AWAY!!! TURN IT OFF!!**

The train ride to France was just lovely.

I have managed to get myself into a bit of a predicament. It was nothing, really, and all's well that ends well, barely worth mentioning, but if you must know, here's what happened:

While walking through the railcars on the way to my seat, I passed by two very **kind and reasonable**[1] businessmen. I accidentally spilled a teensy weensy drop of **water**[2] **near**[3] one gentleman's laptop computer, causing no visible damage **whatsoever**[4]. I immediately apologized for my minor **misstep**[5] and I offered to pay for the entire **thing**[6] because it was, after all, the right thing to do.

1  And by kind and reasonable, I mean angry and short-tempered.
2  Entire mugful of coffee
3  On
4  Causing the entire system to short out
5  I slammed the laptop shut so the man wouldn't notice. He was asleep at the time, did I mention . . . ?
6  I ran away before he woke up.

No wonder they call France the birthplace of French culture.

France is an **absolute dream**! I feel like I'm in another world! Look at that French sign that says *"Départ."* I wonder what it means. Look at that French couple talking. Are they . . . why yes . . . they are talking about wee-wee! Hee-hee, wee-wee!

The **French walls and the French floors are so *exotic***. The walls and floors in England are really quite plain. Nothing to them at all—they just hold the ceiling up. But here! These French walls are so French. There's French culture everywhere as far as the eye can see. And the **best part is—no rain**! Not a drop in sight!

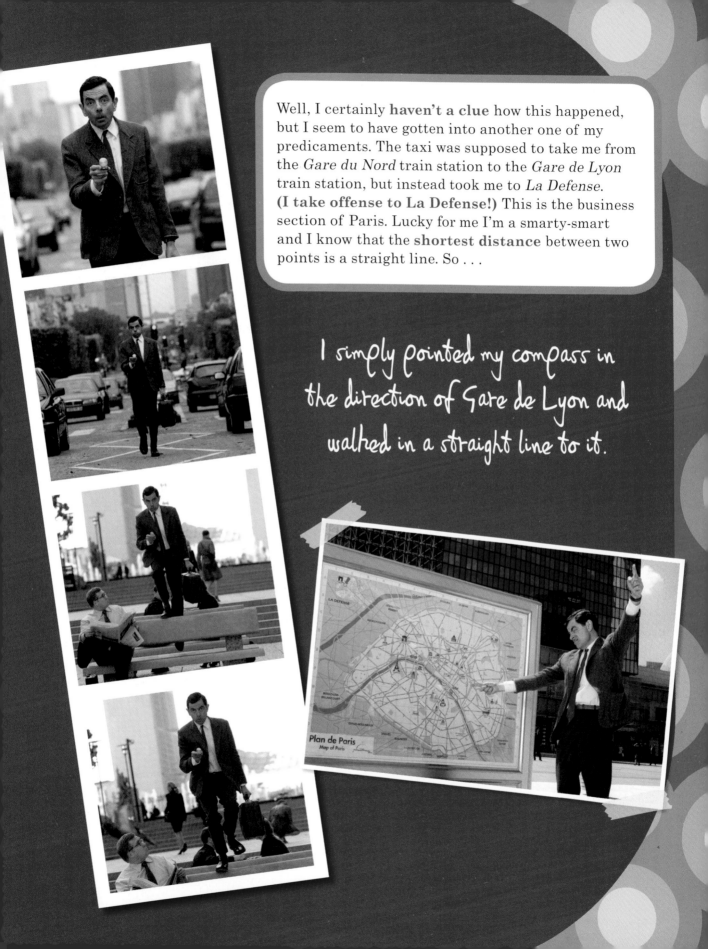

Well, I certainly **haven't a clue** how this happened, but I seem to have gotten into another one of my predicaments. The taxi was supposed to take me from the *Gare du Nord* train station to the *Gare de Lyon* train station, but instead took me to *La Defense*. **(I take offense to La Defense!)** This is the business section of Paris. Lucky for me I'm a smarty-smart and I know that the **shortest distance** between two points is a straight line. So . . .

I simply pointed my compass in the direction of Gare de Lyon and walked in a straight line to it.

Plan de Paris
Map of Paris

Gare de Lyon     Paris, Fran[c]

~~Dear Jack Chirack~~
~~Dear Zhock Sheroek~~
~~Dear Mr. Shellac~~

Dear Leader of France,

How are you? I am *magnifique.* I apologize that I haven't time right now to discuss wee-wee as is customary in your fine country; however, I think you'll understand once you hear what I have to say. There is a very urgent matter of national security that requires your attention.

There are evil, vile, very *très* bad tie-nabbing machines masquerading as vending machines for baguettes situated about your country. I had a run-in with one at the *Gare de Lyon.* Just as I was about to get on one of your trains, I began feeling hungry. I decided to get a baguette from the nearby vending machine. I put *mon* money into the slot and suddenly, the machine nabbed *mon* tie with *mon* neck still in it! I'm sure I don't have to express to you how extremely bad I felt upon being attacked.

So I hope that you will drop everything that you are doing and unplug all the bad machines. Thank you and *gracias.*

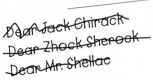

"Get a baguette"— say that ten times fast!

# THE HERO HAS A SETBACK

I've missed the train
So I lose an hour
I wish the next one would
Get here right nower.

Now I must wait
For the next train to arrive
Why oh why
Did the machine eat my tie?

An hour less at the beach
An hour more on my journey
If I don't get there soon
I'm calling an attorney.

This is me missing the blasted train.

# The entire menu was useless.

With about an hour to pass until the next train arrived, I decided to grab a bite to eat—in a proper restaurant this time—not a machine.

How can an Englishman be expected to make sense of words like hors d'oeuvres, entrees, and desserts? There were some things that I figured I'd better steer clear of. I don't know what escargot is, but if it makes the *car go* then it's probably some sort of petrol and I prefer tea. Crepes are another dish on which I passed. Who would want to eat something named after the creeps? Do they taste creepy? And foie gras? Isn't grass for cows?

In the end I let the waiter choose a dish for me. What a mistake that turned out to be . . .

Le Train Bleu    Paris, France

Dear Leader of France,

Mr. Bean here again. I just wanted to add a little something to my last letter if I may, and offer a suggestion to you as leader of this fine country with extraordinary walls.

There is something that will help France attract tourists and make you very rich: cooking school. I don't mean to offend, but your chefs really could stand to learn a thing or two about fine cuisine. Right now they're serving petrol and grass. The waiter at the restaurant at *Gare de Lyon* brought me a plate of something called *fruits de mer* and, as you can see from these photos, it wasn't fruit at all! Or perhaps it was, but it had gone rotten.

I've enclosed a sample of fine British cooking for your enjoyment. It's Teddy's own shepherd's pie and the recipe is famous all over ~~England~~ London my apartment. It's very easy to make. You just start with some minced lamb, then add potatoes and cheese, and keep building like that until eventually you end up with shepherd's pie. You can't help it.

Adios,

Mr. Bean

Please remove all the unpronounceable items from your menus.

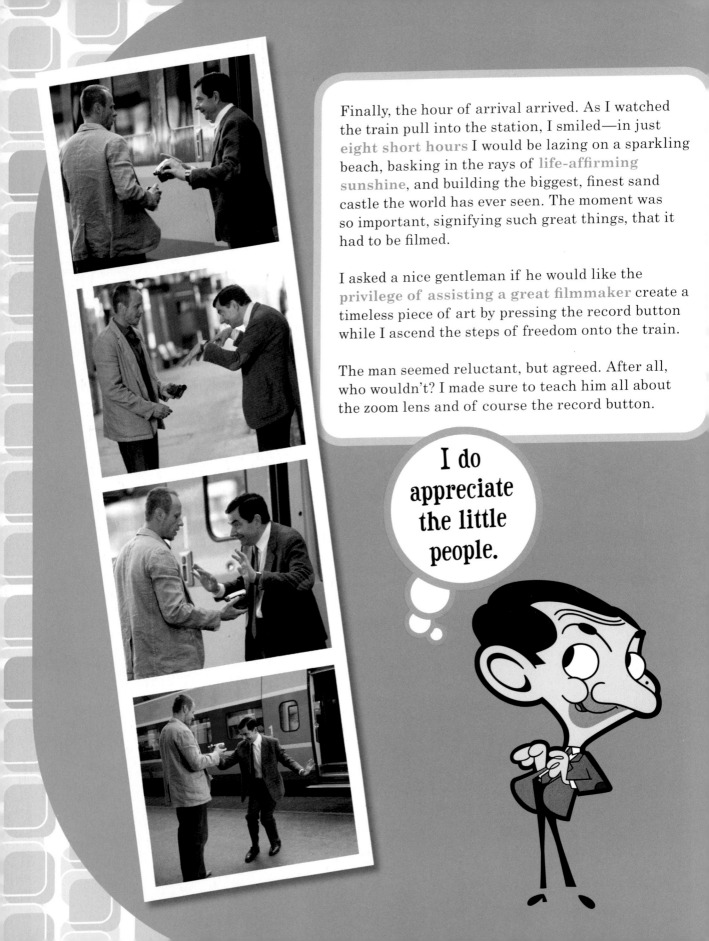

Finally, the hour of arrival arrived. As I watched the train pull into the station, I smiled—in just **eight short hours** I would be lazing on a sparkling beach, basking in the rays of **life-affirming sunshine**, and building the biggest, finest sand castle the world has ever seen. The moment was so important, signifying such great things, that it had to be filmed.

I asked a nice gentleman if he would like the **privilege of assisting a great filmmaker** create a timeless piece of art by pressing the record button while I ascend the steps of freedom onto the train.

The man seemed reluctant, but agreed. After all, who wouldn't? I made sure to teach him all about the zoom lens and of course the record button.

I do appreciate the little people.

After three or four takes, we got the scene.

After recording the **Moment of Ascension** on the Steps to Freedom, the train departed and suddenly I turned round, looked out the window, and who did I see but the gentleman who filmed me running after the train!

You must understand—I do appreciate the little people. After all, who are we without the fans—the dear, sweet little teensy weensy itty bitty tiny winy fans? **But there is only so much of me to go around.** I can't stop and sign autographs for every dear sweet little teensy weensy itty bitty tiny winy fan that wants one—I'd never get a moment's rest!

No, I merely **waved good-bye** as the train left the station and bid him farewell. Perhaps sometime in the future, he will be lucky enough to cross paths with me again.

Gare de Lyon    Paris, France

~~Dear President of Russia~~
~~Dear Boris~~
~~Dear comrade~~

Dear Czar,

Perestroika. I am writing to ask your assistance in a very difficult situation. Borscht.

It seems one of your very famous Russian filmmakers, Emil Dachevsky (who, when I met him I didn't know it was him, because frankly, the bloke didn't even know what a zoom lens was) has left his son, who also appears to be Russian, aboard a train to Cannes.

The boy is going to get off at the next stopsky and wait for his father there, so would you please see to it that they meet upsky? I would do it, but you see I am very pressed for timesky, making my own film about a trip to the beachsky.

The boy is short with short hair and a childlike face. He is very cross with me at the moment for causing his father to miss the train, and he has *nyet* been very nice. I think he needs a time-outsky.

Thank you for attending to this matter, and if there's anything I can do for you, please call my agent because sometimes I'm busy with my gardening.

Stroganoff,

Mr. Bean

Cannes—
that's French.
It's pronounced
"Cannes."

At the next station, the boy, Stefan, got off the train, as his father told him to, but then also helped himself to my camera while he was at it! The train pulled out and I saw him with it, filming me, helpless and unable to get off the moving train. **Nasty little tyke!**

Well, I showed him—I leaped off the train onto the platform and **nearly broke every bone** in my body!

I had to, you see, for my *art*. A filmmaker's camera is his *instrument* and filmmakers without *instruments* are like willows that weep. We are like a dog without a bone. Tea without crumpets. Peanut butter without jelly. Ice cream without pickles. Socks without holes. Fish without bicycles. **Termites without space heaters.** Spectacles without batteries. Very unhappy indeed!

**The little thief!**

Stefan

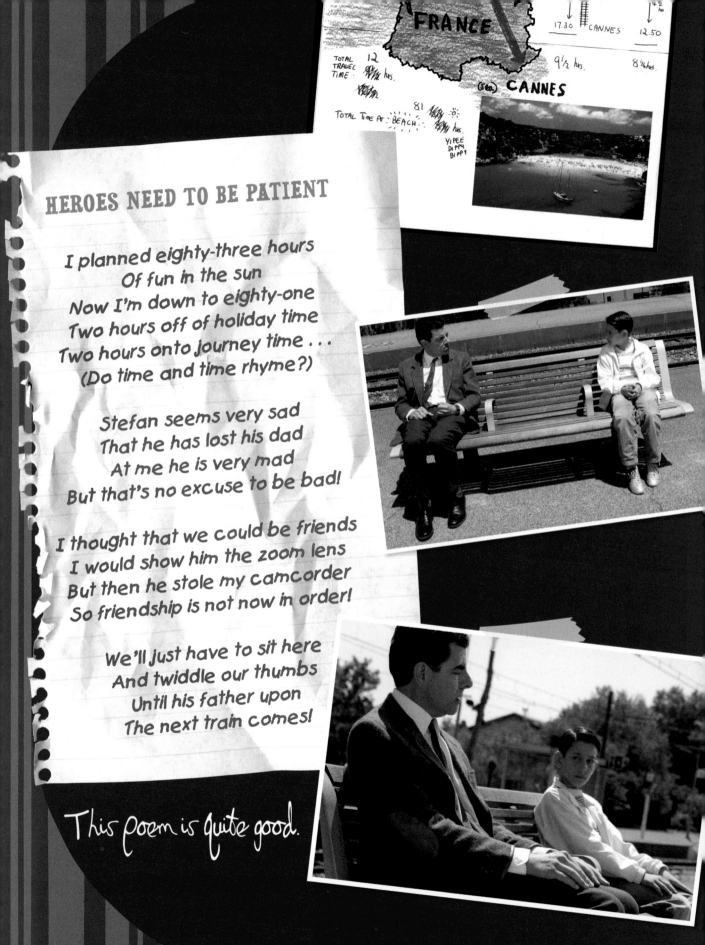

# HEROES NEED TO BE PATIENT

I planned eighty-three hours
Of fun in the sun
Now I'm down to eighty-one
Two hours off of holiday time
Two hours onto journey time . . .
(Do time and time rhyme?)

Stefan seems very sad
That he has lost his dad
At me he is very mad
But that's no excuse to be bad!

I thought that we could be friends
I would show him the zoom lens
But then he stole my camcorder
So friendship is not now in order!

We'll just have to sit here
And twiddle our thumbs
Until his father upon
The next train comes!

This poem is quite good.

FRANCE

17.30  CANNES  12.50

TOTAL
TRAVEL
TIME:  12
9½ hrs.  8¼ hrs.

CANNES
(Sea)

TOTAL TIME AT BEACH  81  hrs.

YIPEE
DIPPY
DIPPY

Papa Dachevsky

Finally the next train arrived and Stefan rose to greet his dad. We saw him in the window and prepared to board. The expression on his face was quite distressed, and only when the train was halfway through the station did we realize why. **It was not slowing down!**

Papa Dachevsky held up a piece of paper in the window with the number of his mobile phone written on it. **Genius that I am**, I decided to film it with my camera so that I would not forget it. But his fingers were covering up the last two digits! Honestly—first the zoom lens and now this. I'm afraid he's not very bright.

Stefan came up with a **brilliant plan**, however. He wrote down every digit from 00 to 99 on my itinerary, and now all we have to do is call every possible combination of phone numbers until we get it right and his dad answers. **Clever boy!** Must get it from his mother.

There was just one small problem . . .

In order to make phone calls on a public phone, one needs coins. Due to my wallet being lost (don't ask) I had none. Stefan had none as well. So we went on a mission to find some.

Stefan approached a nice-looking lady and said something very heartfelt and sad in Russian, and she gave him three gold coins for it! **This was a wonderful start.**

We found some **gambling machines** inside the train station. You put in coins and then cross your fingers, **hoping for some luck.** Then the machine starts ringing and it gushes out all sorts of coins until you are a millionaire and all your wildest dreams come true. They say it happens all the time and I heard that on the telly so **it must be true!**

Except the machines must have been broken because we didn't get any coins from them. Well, that wasn't fair at all. We stood by, innocently, with our hands in our pockets, minding our own business and **doing nothing at all**[1] when suddenly a bell started ringing and a machine spit out loads of money! The stationmaster spotted us, and even though we were just scooping out the money the machine was kind enough to give us, we thought it best to **make a run for it!**

1   Except hitting, kicking, and tilting the blasted machine

*That's the problem with children — they never have any money.*

# THINGS BEGIN TO LOOK BETTER FOR THE HERO

Eighty-one hours of holiday time
Cut to seventy-three
Twelve hours of journey time
Up to twen and ty[1].

No money, no phone
No papa for Stefan
I began to wonder
If we'd ever get to Cannes.

But then we went a-gambling
I hope I'm not a-rambling

With a handful of coins
We were off on a race
I wish I could run faster
We made silly faces
At the stationmaster!

Ha ha hee hee hoo hoo ho ho
Only a few hundred miles to go!

1  That's "twenty" for those of you who aren't *artistes*!

TOTAL TRAVEL TIME hrs.

20

TOTAL TIME AT BEACH hrs.

73 YIPEE DIPPY BIPPY

The Elvis

After running for our lives from the very mean stationmaster, Stefan and I found ourselves in a market square, where a bus nearby had a sign for Cannes in the window. **Wonderful!** Now all we needed were tickets and more money to buy the tickets.

No worries there. As an *artiste*, **I am accustomed to singing for my supper**. There is something beautiful about presenting your song to the world and then being paid for it in cold, hard cash. I stole a speaker from a street performer, blasted some music, and began to dance.

I danced the chicken and the Elvis. And the riverdance. And some tap-dancing besides. I even threw in a couple of fancy moves from the **ball-lay** section of the *Miss Ermentrude's Learn the Two-Step and Other Social Dances* videos.

Which is why I cannot fathom how **my tip bucket did NOT fill up** with loads of money! Not one coin! Obviously the French don't know the first thing about DANCE!

Utterly brilliant. Truly. Deeply. Madly.

I gave myself several encores and I deserved every one.

My performance was, once again, BRILLIANT! STELLAR! YAHOO!

The next thing that happened took me quite by surprise—but pleasantly so. One of my favorite opera songs, "O mio BabBEANo Caro," began to play over the loudspeaker. Immediately I began to mouth the words.

I grabbed Stefan's sweater and pulled it round my head to play the role of the grief-stricken mother. I thought perhaps since these **French sillies don't like dance**, they might like a bit of play-acting instead. Stefan took the role of my sick, poor boy.

Stefan's performance could have done with some improvements, but still, for a beginner, it wasn't half bad. I am starting to see that we **make a great team**. And what's more, when I passed round my handkerchief at the end, it got loaded with money from appreciative fans!

I haven't a clue what the song is about because **I don't speak Italy-ese**, but I'm fairly certain it revolves around a woman named **Babs** whose son ate some bad cabbage.

**Oh dear, oh dear!**

With the money we made, I purchased two tickets for the **bus to Cannes**. Stefan boarded the bus and took his seat. I was just about to present my ticket when **it blew away**. It landed on the ground where a woman stepped on it and it became stuck to her shoe. Then it got caught under the wheel of a stroller. Then a **chicken** caught hold of it on its foot, and a man grabbed the chicken and loaded it onto a truck full of other chickens, and then they all drove off with my ticket!

Oh dear, oh dear! I had no choice but to follow. That's the life of an *artiste*—always going wherever the wind, er, **chicken**, takes you. Thankfully I was able to **borrow**[1] a bike. People are so generous in France.

1  Take from an old man

Oh, how I miss my Mini car . . .

I didn't know they liked to cycle in France, but I must have seen **about one hundred cyclists that day**. Maybe they were tourists. France gets a lot of tourists each year, but I daresay they could all save so much time and see so much more if they just took a car.

But the good news is that I've been doing my toe-touches and eating my corn flakes every morning for the past three months, so I was able to **zoom past** them all like a rocket. One cyclist in a yellow jersey appeared most distressed upon my cycling by and started to pedal faster. Well, I wasn't having that. That was my ticket to Cannes on that chicken's foot, and no one was going to get to it first but me!

Our hero, after a great bike ride over hills and dales, found himself caught in a world between salvation and poultry.

On one of these thousands of chicken feet lay the ticket to paradise. But which chicken? Don't all problems boil down to one question in the end? Which chicken, indeed . . .

# THE HERO IS LOST

Long road.
Too many chickens.
Tears on the canvas of life.
Empty field—
Nothing to be done.

Our hero is lost.
So he walks silly.
He walks like a chicken.
He waddles like a duck.
He saunters backward.
He limps.
Glides.
Slides.
Skips.
Jumps.
Kicks.
Twirls.
When circumstances get serious,
Our hero, yours truly, gets silly.

**Sabine**

After a wonderful night's sleep in the open air, I felt refreshed and renewed. It's a shame that Stefan and I got separated, but I'm sure the czar got my letter and sent an army to help ensure Stefan's safe passage to Cannes, as requested.

Back to my story . . . I woke to find myself in a glorious village. There was a square, a fountain, buildings the color of honey, men wearing berets, a pretty lady, and accordion music playing softly in the background. Why, this town couldn't have been more French if it had been named Frenchy Frenchville Frencherton!

Was I dreaming? I had seen that lady before, but I couldn't think when or where. I seemed to be experiencing what the French call *day-jar-view*. That's when you are sure you have viewed a jar or something in the daytime once before, but you can't think when or where you viewed it. I had it then, but with the lady—not the jar. Perhaps I was having *day-lady-view*. Yes, that must be it.

**Frenchy Frenchville Frencherton**

# GUNFIRE!

# AN ATTACK!

So there I was, enjoying life in the **French countryside**, when suddenly: Explosion! Gunfire! An attack! A pack of German soldiers sprang out from behind a building and assaulted the lady.

I very **heroically jumped** into action and wrestled them to the ground. But then I heard someone shout "CUUUUUUUT!" and everyone stopped.

At that moment, a **lightbulb went off** in my head. The soldiers weren't **attacking the village** at all. They were just filming a yogurt commercial for the telly. The waitress was helping them get into character. *Well,* I supposed, *I could hardly fault them for that.* **Yogurt is very tasty.** (But I'm not sure what it has to do with soldiers.)

There was **one very shouty-pants man** with a megaphone. He really liked that megaphone. He shouted at everyone this way and that, wagged his finger about, furrowed his brow, and pulled his hair out while **his face turned red** with shouting.

Carson Clay

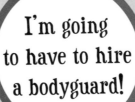

After seeing how **ferocious** I am, they wanted me to star in this commercial. One woman even *begged* me for **my autograph**. She had me sign the bottom of a piece of paper that said **"Waiver"** on top, and then she gave me a wad of cash. I didn't realize how famous I'd become in so short a time.

So I put on a costume and pretended to be the **meanest, ugliest, worst soldier** in the world. The director must have *loved* my work, because after **only one take**, he said I was free to leave. The rest of them had to stay behind and do take after take until they got it right. Perhaps, someday, with practice, **they'll all be as good as me**. Not likely, but possible. I was glad to be done, though. **I'm not an actor**. What I really want to do is direct.

I'm going to have to hire a bodyguard!

So I set off down the road toward Cannes. I wasn't very far when I had another instance of *day-lady-view*! The lady who was working as the waitress in the French village came driving up alongside me on the road in a car that looked **VERY** familiar!

Day-MINI-View!

Our friendship started out well enough. The lady said, **"Blah bleh bleu Cannes?"** To which I responded, "Cannes!" So far, so good.

I showed her my video camera to explain why I was headed to Cannes. Then she said, "Blah bleh bleu *artiste* blah bleh!" so clearly she recognized me as a **famous *artiste*,** which is lucky for her since it would have been quite embarrassing to find out later on, after she'd spent so much time treating me like a *normal* person.

Then, well, then **I just gave up talking** to her because it became awfully, awfully complicated. She started crying **very loudly** and said, "Blah bleh bleu blah *ce* bleh bleu *les* blah bleh *la* blah bleh *mwah mon* bleu." I gathered she was very distressed over the health of her grandmother, who had just had an unfortunate incident with a garden hose. **The poor dear.**

CANNES!

207 UHO 75

## THE HERO IS ANNOYED!

Hours later we're in this café
The lady's been
Sobbing and jabb'ring all day
I've spent sixty-seven hours
Getting from here to there
I long for the sun and the fresh sea air

Now only twenty-eight
Holiday hours remain
And travel has proven to be quite a pain
I don't know what happened with
Her granny's hose
But from the sound of things
I think it went straight up her nose
And for this mishap I do feel very sad
But all this sobbing is driving me mad!!

LET'S GO PLEASE!

I WANT TO GO!
GO GO GO!

## It was glorious!

Just when I was about to **give up hope** of ever getting to Cannes, the most wonderful thing happened. Stefan came running into the café, followed by the street **performers** from the market square!

Stefan explained, as best he could in Russian, where he'd been and what he'd been doing. Apparently he'd been doing lots of **dancing**. One of the buskers began to play the drums and of course they *begged* me to give an encore performance of my earlier **dance recital**! Everyone in the café was up on the tables and countertops. This probably wasn't good—to have people's feet upon the same surfaces people eat on—but with the state of cuisine in this country, I didn't see how it could hurt.

After the **dancing was over**, Stefan and the lady and I set out for Cannes in the Mini. Stefan sat in the backseat and talked a lot in Russian. The lady, whose name I learned was Sabine, sat up front and talked a lot in French. I sat up front and said **"wee,"** just to be polite.

For three people who **did not understand** one another at all, we had ourselves quite a lively conversation! Sabine would say, "Blah bleh bleu," and Stefan would reply, "Blahsky, blah-poff, blah-nik," and I would say, "Wee." I was glad to see that **everyone was getting along**. The worst was behind us, and Cannes was only a car ride away.

What could possibly go wrong now?

## STOP SAYING WHAT COULD POSSIBLY GO WRONG!!!

Note to self: Something ALWAYS goes wrong! Especially to me. **Oh dear, oh dear . . .**

Sabine saw on the telly that I am wanted for kidnapping! Can you believe it? Stefan's dad is looking for him, and the mean old grumpy stationmaster saw us together, so they're saying that **I stole Stefan**! This all started because Stefan stole *my* camera, if you remember.

But still, I've got to return that boy to his father as quickly as possible and I do mean **fast fast fast**! Then I will go to the beach, Sabine will go do whatever it is she's doing in Cannes, Stefan will be with his parents at last, and this whole mess will be sorted out.

Finding Stefan's dad will be very easy, thankfully. It seems he is going to be at some sort of film festival in Cannes—they said so on the telly. He's a member of the jury. How irritating to be called for jury duty in a whole other country. **I wonder how one juries over a film. I** suppose the boring ones go to jail and the lively ones are set free.

# WANTED
## MINISTERE DE LA SECURITE
DIRECTION GENERALE DE LA SECURITE NATIONALE
DIRECTION CENTRALE DE LA POLICE

### LA POLICE RECHERCHE CET HOMME

Auteur présumé de l'enlèvement de Stefan Dachevsky

Appelez au

**04 93 96 92 53**

We were famous in the wrong way.

In order to get to the film festival, we had to get past the guards. Luckily, Sabine had a golden ticket. I don't know how she managed to get that as a waitress, but it really helped us.

At the gates, we came up with a master plan to get the rest of us in. Stefan put on a wig and sunglasses so as not to be recognized, and I put a sweater round my head. After all, our faces were all over the telly—we were famous-but-in-the-wrong-way. I reprised my role as Babs, the mother of the bad-cabbage-eater. Sabine said to the security man, "Blah bleh bleu," which I'm guessing meant something to the effect of, "This is my poor dear grandmother who has just had an unfortunate incident with a garden hose, this is my child who's eaten some bad cabbage, and I have a ticket so would you kindly let us pass without any trouble, complications, or questions, please?" And he did!

Inside the auditorium, there was a film showing and a **very glamorous audience** wearing gloves and sparkly dresses. Stefan peeked through the curtains and spotted his mum and dad. I told him that when the film was over, he could go running out to greet them. We said our **good-byes** and I slipped out the back. It was FINALLY time for the beach!

Cannes Film Festival    Cannes, France

Dear Czar,

I've returned the boy to his papa, no thanks to you. Where were your troops? Must I do everything by myself?

Anyway, I take back what I said about Stefan before. He is very nice and very agreeable indeed. I hope to come to Russia one day and visit him. Could you please give me directions? I know to leave Europe and turn right, but then if you could just talk me through the rest of the way I would greatly appreciate it.

Thanksky,

Mr. Bean

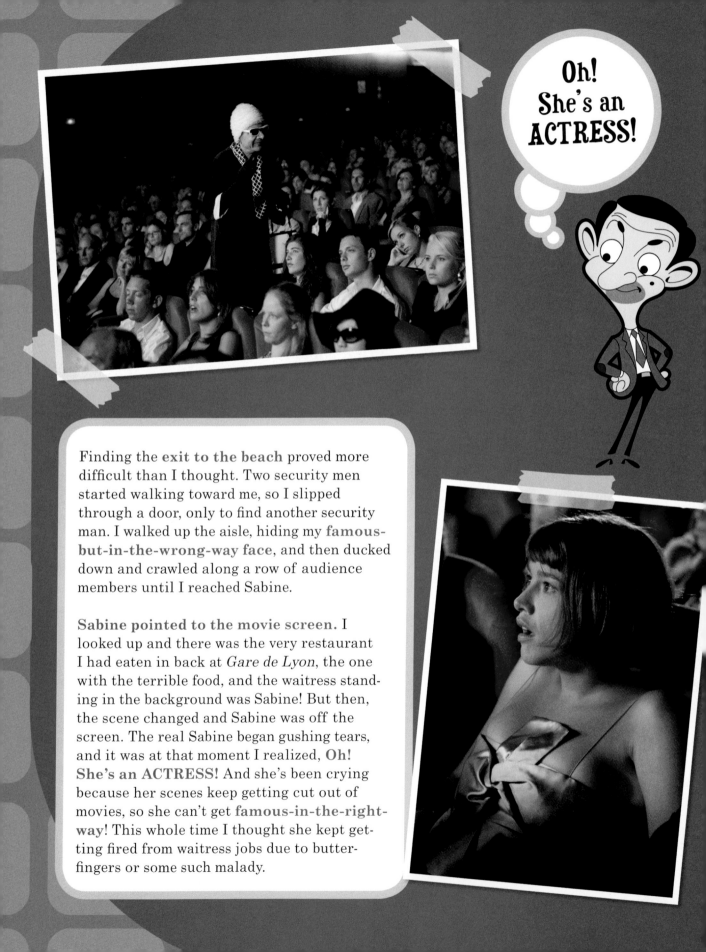

Oh! She's an ACTRESS!

Finding the **exit to the beach** proved more difficult than I thought. Two security men started walking toward me, so I slipped through a door, only to find another security man. I walked up the aisle, hiding my **famous-but-in-the-wrong-way face**, and then ducked down and crawled along a row of audience members until I reached Sabine.

**Sabine pointed to the movie screen.** I looked up and there was the very restaurant I had eaten in back at *Gare de Lyon*, the one with the terrible food, and the waitress standing in the background was Sabine! But then, the scene changed and Sabine was off the screen. The real Sabine began gushing tears, and it was at that moment I realized, **Oh! She's an ACTRESS!** And she's been crying because her scenes keep getting cut out of movies, so she can't get **famous-in-the-right-way**! This whole time I thought she kept getting fired from waitress jobs due to butter-fingers or some such malady.

Sabine's crying drew much attention from the security men, so I had to duck and run. At the back of the auditorium I slipped through an open door. I was in the **projection room**. The film currently showing was **boooooooring!** It was one of those pieces of rubbish directed by Mr. Shouty-Pants—the one making the yogurt commercial with all those soldiers. If I were a part of the jury like Stefan's dad, I'd find this movie guilty and sentence it to **infinity years in prison!**

Well, I have lots of footage of Sabine from our travels, and if she wants to be up on that big screen, then up on the big screen she shall be. I plugged in my *instrument*, I pressed play, and there she was.

The sound of **Mr. Shouty-Pants's** movie was still playing so you heard, "Without you I am nothing, and the world is nothing . . ." while you saw Sabine standing in the square in **Frenchy Frenchville Frencherton**. Then you heard, "How can I live, knowing that you've found another?" And I showed some scenes of myself— eating the rotten **fruits de mer**, walking silly, et cetera.

**It was BRILLIANT!** It was so entertaining and you laughed and you cried and you learned about yourself and it was better than the best movie ever made, which up until now was *Curious George*, but now it's **Sabine and Bean**, which is even better because it RHYMES!

## HOORAY!!

Then I ran into **problems with the film**. It started coming apart, and I'm not sure but I smelled something burning. There was a banging at the door and a **grand commotion**. I ran through the only **open door I could find**[1] and ended up back in the auditorium with the security men and **Mr. Shouty-Pants** chasing me and wagging his finger. Then I got up onstage and Stefan's dad told everyone that I kidnapped his son!

1 Climbed out the projection-room window, stepping on a few audience members' heads

*But just when I thought I was done for . . .*

Stefan came running out and told his father that I was **not a terrible kidnapper**, but rather his friend! The whole audience applauded, the security men left me alone, and Sabine was congratulated by very important film people and **took her place among the stars**. You would think I would have been happy, right? Well, I wasn't. You know why? Stefan had said, literally, and I quote, "No! He is my friend!" **IN ENGLISH!**

"You speak English?" I asked.

"Of course!" he replied.

Dear Czar,

Forget all those nice things I said about Stefan. He's a sly little trickster after all and he could speak English the entire time-sky!

Mr. Bean

# THE HERO SUCCEEDS!

In all the excitement I almost forgot
To go to the beach
With the time that I've got
Only half an hour left until home I return
But that's all right because
Too much sun causes burn.

Thirty minutes will be grand
We'll build castles in the sand
I'll play with my friends
Until the day comes to an ends.

This journey has lasted
Eighty-three hours
Almost time to return to
England's showers.
But I'll look back with lots of
Smiles and cheer
Because the real fun's been
In traveling here!

# Sand

### Pros:

You can build castles with it and just a bit of water.
You can bury yourself in it, which is great fun.
Sand also makes the beach very sparkly and nice.

### Cons:

When it gets inside your swim trunks it is most uncomfortable.
Also, **HOT FEET!**

I had a fun time on the beach. I even forgave Stefan for not telling me he spoke English.

# What I Learned During My Trip to France
## by Mr. Bean

1. Some soldiers just want to eat yogurt and make commercials.

2. Beware of French tie-eating machines.

3. Gambling machines are always lucky if you tilt them just right.

4. Leave the window open so Teddy can get some fresh air.

5. Chickens always lead to more chickens.

6. When things get serious, you must be silly.

7. You don't really need to learn to speak French if you're going to France. Just wee-wee your way through the entire country. I did, and had a wonderful time!